CW00865589

For my incredible daughters Elle and Sophia.

Thank you to my one of a kind husband.

Butterfly Bridge

Jess Turner

Illustrated by

Stephen Stone

When Elle and Sophia fall asleep something magical happens, they travel to wonderful places in their dreams.

Tonight, when the girls close their eyes, they float away to Butterfly Bridge.

Elle and Sophia arrive in their dreams to a beautiful bridge, where all butterflies meet once they have hatched from their cocoons.

The butterflies travel to this bridge to test their new wings, and to learn to be calm and kind through meditation.

Elle and Sophia have also been transformed and now have wonderful wings of their own.

Brontë, the most experienced butterfly, welcomes

Elle and Sophia and teaches them how to fly.

Brontë encourages the new butterflies to be brave
and kind to one another.

Elle and Sophia join the butterflies flying off the bridge.
They glide over the glistening water, and up through the
tall trees.

Elle and Sophia learn to fly high, low, backwards, forwards and even upside down.

They twirl and zigzag across the sky.
They take it in turns and they celebrate each
other's success.

'**Om...Om...Om...**' The loud calming sounds began.

Brontë said *'The meditation is about to begin.'*

All the butterflies including Elle and Sophia, find a

comfortable place to sit.

The ground is covered in beautiful butterflies of all colours and sizes.

Each day the butterflies take turns to lead the meditation. Today it is Bipin's turn to lead.

'Close your eyes.

Take three deep breaths...**One**...**Two**...**Three**...

Imagine that there is a warm light shining on your body.

It starts at the bottom of your body and is slowly working its way up to your head, and to the tips of your wings.

Now as you breathe in, think in your head the words, **I AM**,

and as you breathe out, think the words **BRAVE**,

breathe in, think, **I AM**, and as you breathe out, think **CALM**,

breathe in, think, **I AM**, and as you breathe out think, **KIND**,

breathe in, think, **I AM**, and as you breathe out think, **LISTENING**.'

'Now bring your attention back to your body.

What can you hear?

What do you feel?'

Now let's say one more **Om** all together.
Ommmmmmm

Bring your wings together in humble gratitude and we all say together **'Namaste'.**

Brontë explained 'Namaste is a greeting, which means we bow to each other. It is used to recognise the goodness in each other.'

It was nearly time to go, but Elle and Sophia had time for one more flight. They felt brave for trying something new and still so calm from the meditation.

Elle and Sophia arrive back in their beds, feeling brave, calm and so grateful for the kindness the other butterflies had shown them.

They fall back into a deep, happy sleep.

REFLECTION QUESTIONS:

What do you think Elle and Sophia learnt in their dreams?

What made Elle and Sophia feel calm? What makes you feel calm?

How were the butterflies and the girls kind?

What could you do to be kind?

How were Elle and Sophia brave? When were you last brave and how did it make you feel?

LESSONS LEARNT:

To be brave, which means ready to face new things or pain.

To be calm, which means to be quiet and still; not showing strong emotions.

To be kind, which means being helpful and friendly.

Butterfly Bridge
First published in 2021 by
Jess Turner

Text © Jess Turner 2021
www.instagram.com/readfeedplaylove

Illustration © Stephen Stone 2021
www.yellowstonestudio.co.uk

A CIP catalogue record for this book is available
from the British Library.
ISBN 9798561906244 (pbk)

Printed in Great Britain
by Amazon